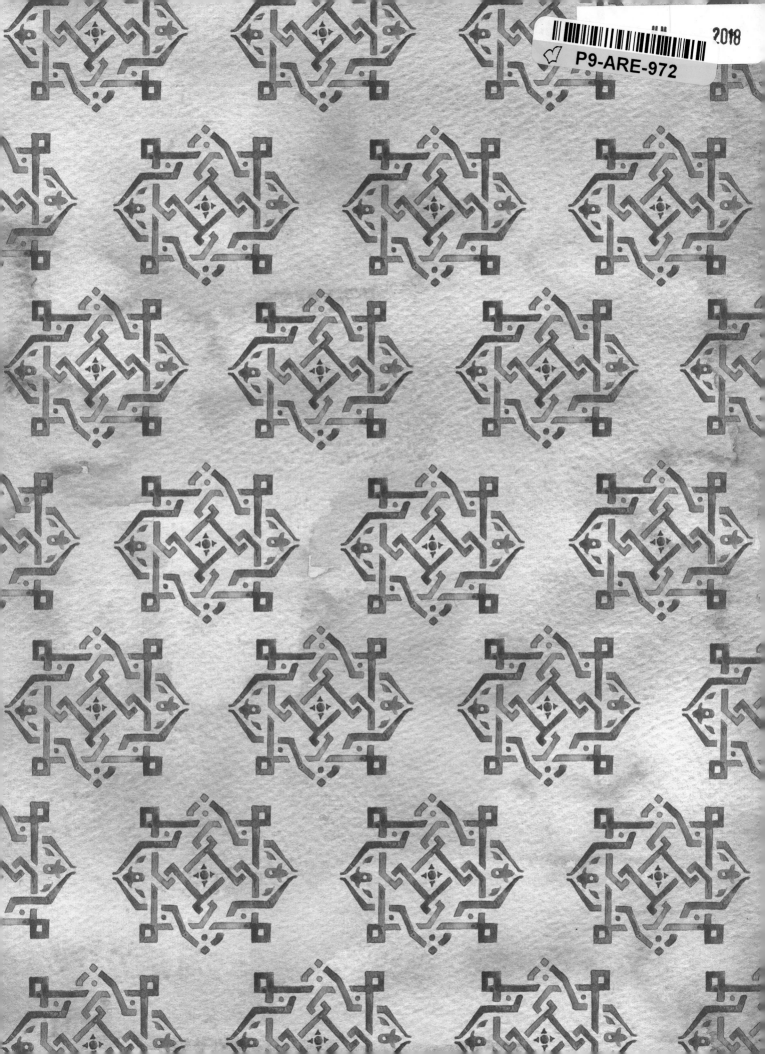

P9-ARE-972

2018

Time To Pray

أوقات الصلاة

MAHA ADDASI

Arabic Translation by Nuha Albitar

Illustrated by
NED GANNON

BOYDS MILLS PRESS
Honesdale, Pennsylvania

Text copyright © 2010 by Maha Addasi
Arabic translation copyright © 2010 by Nuha Albitar
Illustrations copyright © 2010 by Ned Gannon
All rights reserved

Boyds Mills Press, Inc.
815 Church Street
Honesdale, Pennsylvania 18431
Printed in the United States of America

Library of Congress Cataloging-in-Publication Data

Addasi, Maha, 1968-
Time to pray / Maha Addasi ; illustrated by Ned B. Gannon. — 1st ed.
p. cm.
Summary: When young Yasmin goes for a visit, her grandmother teaches her a
Muslim's daily prayers, makes special prayer clothes, and gives a gift that will
help Yasmin remember when to pray. Includes facts about prayer customs.
ISBN 978-1-59078-611-6 (hardcover : alk. paper)
[1. Prayer—Fiction. 2. Islam—Customs and practices—Fiction. 3. Muslims—
Fiction. 4. Grandmothers—Fiction.] I. Gannon, Ned, ill. II. Title.
PZ7.A237Tim 2010   [E]—dc22
2010005090

First edition
The text of this book is set in 13-point Lucida Bright.
The illustrations are done in oils.

10 9 8 7 6 5 4 3 2

R0452436366

To my children, Serena, Diana, Samer,
and Ramzy, with love
—*M.A.*

To Meg and family
—*N.G.*

IN THE DARKNESS, green lights winked at me from the minaret of the nearby mosque. I heard the voice of the *muezzin* calling, "Come to pray, come to pray." It was my first night at Grandma's house.

I learned that the muezzin calls Muslims to prayer five times each day. But when I heard the call, I was too tired. I closed my eyes until the light from the hall bathroom lit my room.

كانت ليلتي الأولى في بيتِ جدّتي، وكان الظلام حالكًا ثم وَمضَ ضوءٌ أخضر،
عرفتُ أنه منبعث من المئذنة العالية التابعة للمسجد المجاور. وحيثُ أُقيم لا يوجد
مسجد.

ثم سمعتُ صوت المؤذن الذي يدعو المسلمين للصلاة خمس مرات كل يوم.
ردّدَ المؤذن حيّ على الصلاة، حيّ على الصلاة، ولكنني كنت متعبة جدًا
فغلبني النوم. ثم أضيئت غرفتي من ضوء الحمام.

Grandma stood near the sink. I watched her wash her hands, mouth, nose, face, and arms. She ran a damp hand over her hair and her ears. Then she washed her feet.

The muezzin called, "Prayer is better than sleep. Prayer is better than sleep." But, as much as I tried, I could not keep my eyes open.

لقد استيقظت جدتي فأخذت أراقبها

وهي تقف بجانب المغسلة ثم وهي تغسل يديها وفمها وأنفها ثم وجهها وذراعيها، ثم

تمسح رأسها وأذنيها، وغسلت قدميها أيضاً، ردد المؤذن " الصلاة خيرٌ من النوم" ،

"الصلاةُ خيرٌ من النوم" ولكنني لم أنجح في أن أبقى مستيقظة.

"I heard the muezzin," I told Grandma at breakfast. "But I was too sleepy to get up."

"You are still young, Yasmin, *habibti*," Grandma said, flattening the dough for cinnamon rolls. "With practice, you'll be able to rise early."

"But, Teta," I said, calling Grandma by my favorite name for her, "we don't have a mosque near my home. How will I ever know when to pray?"

Grandma's eyes smiled at me. "We'll figure a way, habibti," she said as she placed the rolls on a tray. I like it when Teta calls me habibti, my love. "In fact, I know how we will spend our morning."

في الصباح وأثناء

الأفطار أخبرت جدتي بأنني سمعت المؤذن وبأنني كنت شديدة النعاس ولم أستطع أن أستيقظ. كانت جدتي تعد لنا لفائف القرفة فقالت لي وهي تعجنها بيديها، أنك لا زلت صغيرة يا ياسمين ولكنك بالممارسة ستستطيعين أن تنهضي مبكرة.

كلمة تيتا من أحب الأسماء لديَّ لمخاطبة جدتي.

فقلت لها تيتا ولكن لا يوجد مسجد حيث نسكن ، فكيف أعرف أوقات الصلاة؟

لمعت عينا جدتي وابتسمت ، بينما كانت تصنع اللفائف في الصينية ثم قالت لي: حبيبتي سوف نرى طريقة لذلك. شعرت بالسعادة عندما نادتني جدتي بحبيبتي فهي الكلمة المفضلة عندي.

ثم قالت جدتي الآن عرفت أين سنقضي صباحنا.

Soon we were on our way. Our first stop was at a fabric store. "What color fabric would you like, Yasmin?" Teta asked. "I will make you some special prayer clothes."

It took me a while to decide. There were many pretty designs. Finally, I pointed to a bolt of fabric high up on a shelf. "I like that one the best, Teta," I said. The vendor unrolled the material and cut two yard's length.

وفي الحال كنا في الطريق.

محطتنا الأولى كانت متجر للأقمشة ، وهناك سألتني جدتي: ما هو اللون الذي تفضلينه يا ياسمين؟ لأنني سأخيط لك بعض الملابس الخاصة للصلاة. أخذت برهة لأقرر إذ كان هناك كثير من التصاميم الجميلة. وأخيرا أشرت إلى الرف العلوي وقلت لتيتا لقد أحببت ذلك القماش كثيرا.

بسط البائع القماش وقص لنا ياردين.

Next we stopped at the corner store where Teta helped me pick out a small rug. I ran my hand over several of them. They were soft and velvety, with beautiful patterns. I settled on one with blue swirls and crescents.

"This will be your special prayer rug, my Yasmin," Teta said.

محطتنا الثانية كانت على زاوية المتجر في المكان الذي أستطيع أن أختار سجادة صغيرة للصلاة. مررت بيدي على مجموعة من السجاد وكانت قطع السجاد ناعمة وذات ملمس مخملي ونقشات جميلة. ثم استقر رأيي على السجادة التي لها دوامات زرقاء وأهله صغيرة. هنا قالت لي تيتا:هذه السجادة ستكون سجادتك الخاصة يا ياسمينتي.

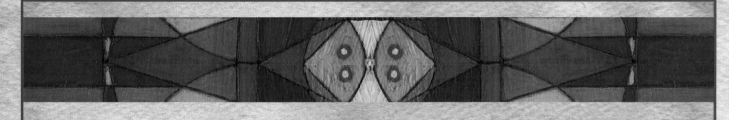

At our last stop, Teta left the store with a small cardboard box. As I was about to ask her what was inside, the muezzin began crooning the call to prayer. It was the second prayer of the day.

"We need to get home so I can pray the afternoon prayer," Teta said.

Many storekeepers locked their shops and walked to the mosque. A vendor who had a pyramid of oranges on his sidewalk juice stand spread a blanket over the fruit and hurried off to pray.

"Can we go to the mosque, too?" I asked.

"I'll take you there for the late-afternoon prayer," Teta said. "It might be less busy during the third prayer of the day."

في نهاية جولتنا ابتاعت تيتا صندوق كرتوني صغير، لم أعرف ماذا كان بداخله، وكنت على وشك أن أسألها لكن المؤذن كان قد بدأ يدعو إلى الصلاة. كان وقت الصلاة الثانية لذلك اليوم فقالت جدتي: علينا أن نذهب إلى البيت لكي أصلي صلاة الظهر.

كثير من أصحاب المتاجر أغلقوا متاجرهم ومشوا إلى المسجد.

البائع الذي كان لديه هرماً من البرتقال وعصارة فواكه على الرصيف، غطى الفواكه بحرام من عنده وهرع للصلاة.

سألَت ياسمين : هل نستطيع أن نذهب نحن أيضاً؟ قالت جدتي: سوف آخذك لصلاة العصر، حيث يكون الازدحام أقل في الصلاة الثالثة عادة.

At home, Teta taught me how to wash before praying.
I did not have the proper clothes for prayer, but Teta said it was
all right. Teta stood for some time before she bent forward at the
waist and placed her hands on her knees. She went down on her
knees, then rested her forehead on the ground. I watched as she
did this several times. Then Teta sat up and turned her palms
upward. Her mouth moved all the time. It was fun to watch.

وفي البيت، علمتني جدتي كيف أتوضأ للصلاة، ثم وقفت بجانبها وهي تصلي.

لم يكن لدي الملابس الخاصة للصلاة ولكن تيتا قالت لي لا بأس.

راقبت جدتي وهي تركع وتسجد وتحرك فمها طول الوقت ثم جلست ورفعت

كفيها للأعلى. كان منظرها ممتعا.

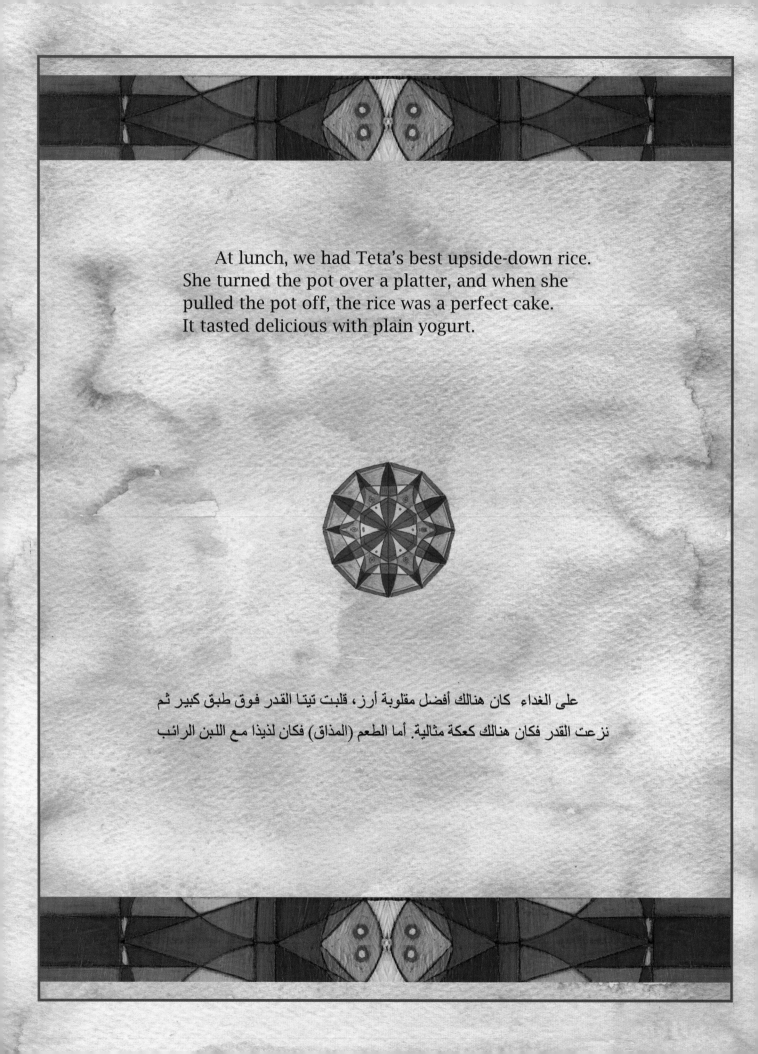

At lunch, we had Teta's best upside-down rice.
She turned the pot over a platter, and when she
pulled the pot off, the rice was a perfect cake.
It tasted delicious with plain yogurt.

على الغداء كان هنالك أفضل مقلوبة أرز، قلبت تيتا القدر فوق طبق كبير ثم

نزعت القدر فكان هنالك كعكة مثالية. أما الطعم (المذاق) فكان لذيذا مع اللبن الرائب

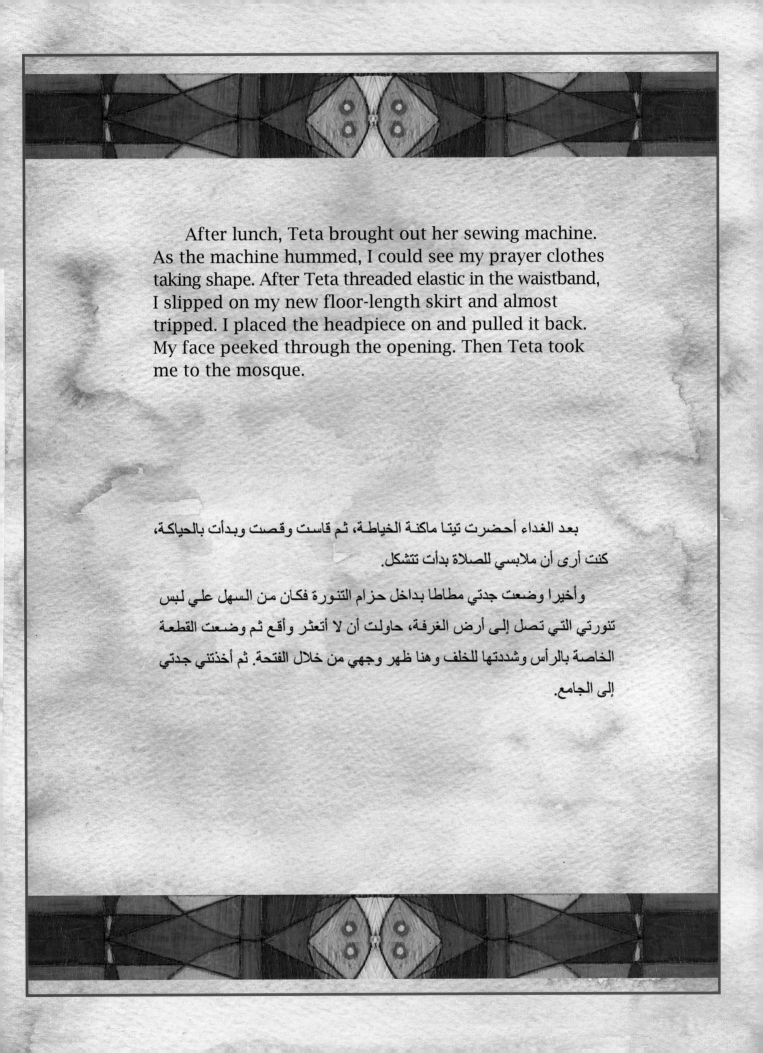

After lunch, Teta brought out her sewing machine. As the machine hummed, I could see my prayer clothes taking shape. After Teta threaded elastic in the waistband, I slipped on my new floor-length skirt and almost tripped. I placed the headpiece on and pulled it back. My face peeked through the opening. Then Teta took me to the mosque.

بعد الغداء أحضرت تيتا ماكنة الخياطة، ثم قاست وقصت وبدأت بالحياكة، كنت أرى أن ملابسي للصلاة بدأت تتشكل.

وأخيرا وضعت جدتي مطاطا بداخل حزام التنورة فكان من السهل علي لبس تنورتي التي تصل إلى أرض الغرفة، حاولت أن لا أتعثر وأقع ثم وضعت القطعة الخاصة بالرأس وشددتها للخلف وهنا ظهر وجهي من خلال الفتحة. ثم أخذتني جدتي إلى الجامع.

I sat on the floor with Teta in one of the back rows. I was surprised that the muezzin did not go all the way to the top of the minaret. He called through a microphone instead!

دهشت عندما وجدت أن المؤذن لا يصعد إلى قمة المئذنة، بل بدلا من ذلك كان

يؤذن عبر مذياع كبير

Over the next few days, Teta helped me practice my prayers. We prayed together a few more times before I left for home. I especially liked the fourth prayer at sunset. The sky always had swirls of red, even when there were no clouds.

The last and fifth prayer of the day came just before my bedtime when it was very dark outside. I knew I would miss the twinkling minaret lights outside my window.

بعد أسبوع كان عليّ العودة إلى بيتي، تمرنت خلاله مع تيتا عدة مرات على الصلاة.

أنا شخصيا أحببت الصلاة الرابعة عند الغروب (صلاة المغرب) حيث تكون السماء موشحة بالشفق الأحمر حتى وإن لم يكن هناك غيوم.

أما الصلاة الخامسة (صلاة العشاء) فكانت قبل موعد نومي حيث الظلام يكون حالكًا في الخارج. هنالك تأكدت بأنني سأفتقد الومضات المضيئة الخضراء المنبعثة من المئذنة.

When it was time to leave, Teta took me to the
airport. I gave her a big hug.
"Thank you, my teta," I said.
"I will miss you, habibti," she said.
We are very close, my teta and I.

في المطار احتضنت تيتا بشدة وهي أيضا احتضنتني بشدة وقلت لها شكرا لك
يا تيتا.

قالت تيتا: سوف افتقدك يا حبيبتي. لقد كنت مقربة جدا من تيتا.

When I returned home, Mom helped me unpack. My little brother took my prayer clothes and put them with his toys. He made a perfect train tunnel out of my skirt and turned my headpiece into a little tent. Mom helped me put my prayer clothes in a safe place.

Then I saw it—the box that Teta carried home from the market. I could not believe my eyes! Inside was a miniature mosque.

"Wow," Mom said. "This is a special prayer clock."

Dad helped me set the timer for the five prayers of the day. When it went off, it didn't ring. Instead, it made the sound of the muezzin calling us to prayer.

لا زلت لا أعرف ماذا بداخل الصندوق الذي غلفته تيتا.

في بيتي وعندما أردت أن أفتح الصندوق صرف انتباهي أخي الصغير. فقد كانت معه ملابسي الخاصة للصلاة.

كانت التنورة كنفق مناسب للقطار، أما قطعة الرأس فقد أصبحت خيمة.

ثم ساعدتني أمي على وضع أشيائي الخاصة في مكان آمن.

وأخيرا فتحنا الصندوق، لم أستطع أن أصدق عينيّ. كان فيه مسجد مصغر.

دهشت أمي وقالت:هذه ساعة خاصة للصلاة. أما أنا فكنت مبتهجة جدا، ثم ساعدني والدي في ضبط الساعة على الصلوات الخمس.هذه الساعة لا ترن بل بدلا من ذلك يعلو صوت المؤذن يدعونا إلى الصلاة.

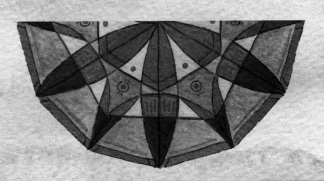

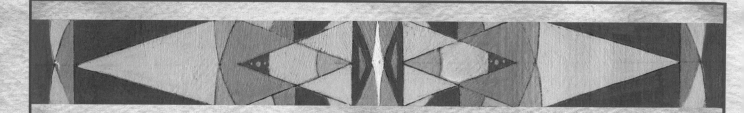

Now when I walk by the cinnamon bun store at
the mall, it smells like Teta's house. When Mom makes
upside-down rice, it may not look like Teta's, but it tastes
like Teta's. And when the prayer clock goes off, it sounds
just like the muezzin near Teta's house.

I don't always pray all five prayers. I'm still practicing.
Sometimes when the prayer clock rings before dawn,
I turn over and go back to sleep.

But don't tell Teta!

الآن كلما أمر بجانب مخيز لفائف القرفة أشم رائحة بيت جدتي، وعندما تصنع

لنا والدتي المقلوبة ومع أنها ليست كمقلوبة تيتا إلا أنني أشعر وكأنني في بيت تيتا.

حتى الآن لا أداوم على الصلوات الخمس فأنا لا زلت أتمرن وأحيانا وقبل صلاة

الفجر اتقلب في السرير وأعود للنوم هس لا تخبر تيتا.

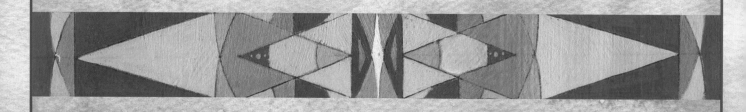

Prayer Times

Practicing Muslims pray five times each day. Prayer reminds Muslims, spiritually and mentally, about the ultimate purpose of life. As Muslims stand to pray, they must face what is known as the *Qibla* (kib-LA). This is an Arabic word for the direction in which Muslims must face when they pray. Wherever they are in the world, Muslims face in the direction of the most sacred site in Islam, a cube-shaped building called the *Ka'bah*, which stands in Mecca, Saudi Arabia. Many prayer rugs now have small compasses attached to them that show the direction of Mecca from anyplace a Muslim chooses to pray.

Muslims do not need to be in a *masjid* (mas-JID), or mosque, to pray. They believe that any clean spot on earth is suitable for prayer, so that the entire world is one masjid.

Specific prayer times occur during the day. A man called the *muezzin* (moo-EZZ-in) calls people for each prayer. In places where there are no mosques, people set special prayer clocks or download prayer clocks onto their computers to remind them of each prayer time. Before praying, Muslims perform a special washing ritual, or ablution, called *wudu*. Prayer is not valid without this.

Each prayer takes its name from the Arabic word for part of the day.

One: *Fajr* (FA-jr), or dawn, actually performed just before dawn. In fact, it is specified that if there is enough natural light outside for a person to distinguish between a black thread and a white thread, then it is too late for the Fajr prayer. Muslims are forbidden to pray as the sun rises, when the sun is at its peak in the sky at noon, and when the sun is setting. The sun is only a guide to the time of day.

Two: *Zuhr* (ZOO-hor), performed anytime after twelve noon until the time for the next prayer in the late afternoon.

Three: *Asr* (A-ser), or afternoon, performed in the late afternoon, when an object's shadow is twice its length. This prayer can be performed up to the time before the sun begins to set.

Four: *Maghrib* (Ma-GH-rib), or sunset, performed after the sun sets completely, up until the last light in the sky is gone.

Five: *Isha* (I-sha), or evening, performed anytime from the end of dusk until just before dawn, or the Fajr prayer time.

These five prayers are called *Fard* prayers, meaning they are required prayers. Muslims are strongly urged to perform other prayers. And additional prayers are recommended because they were performed by the Prophet Mohammad. Muslims strive to live their lives the way the Prophet did.

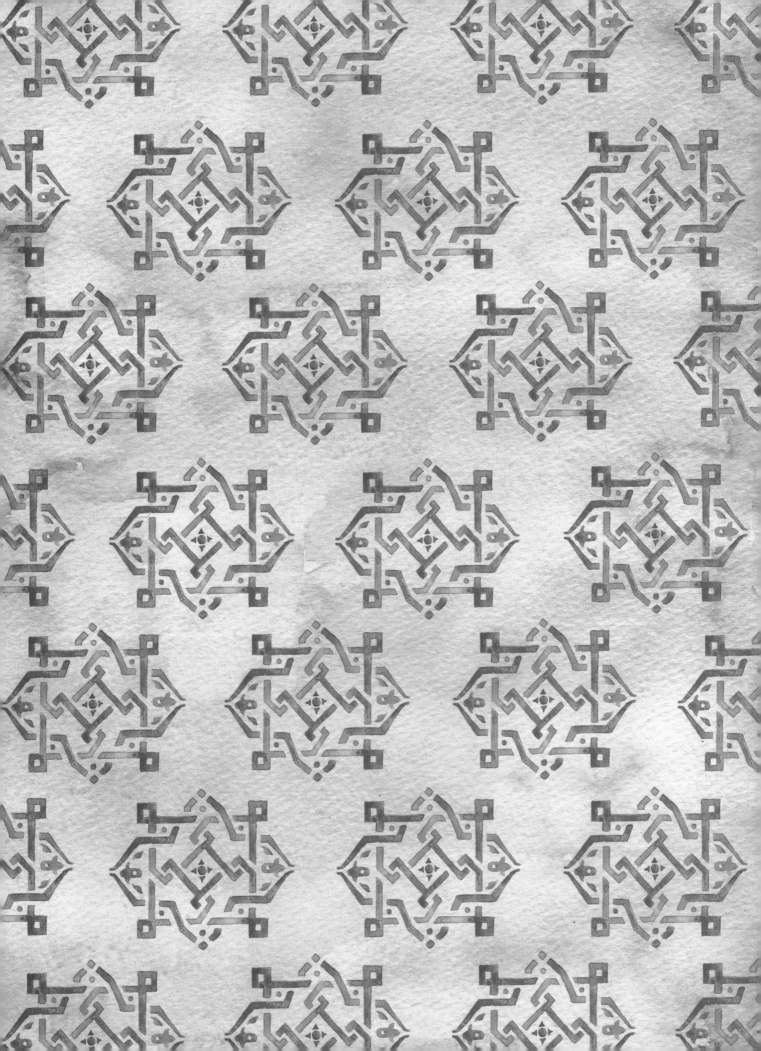